Best Fishes!

Dan Hanna

The Pout-Pout Fish and the Bully-Bully Shark

Deborah Diesen

Pictures by Dan Hanna

Farrar Straus Giroux • New York

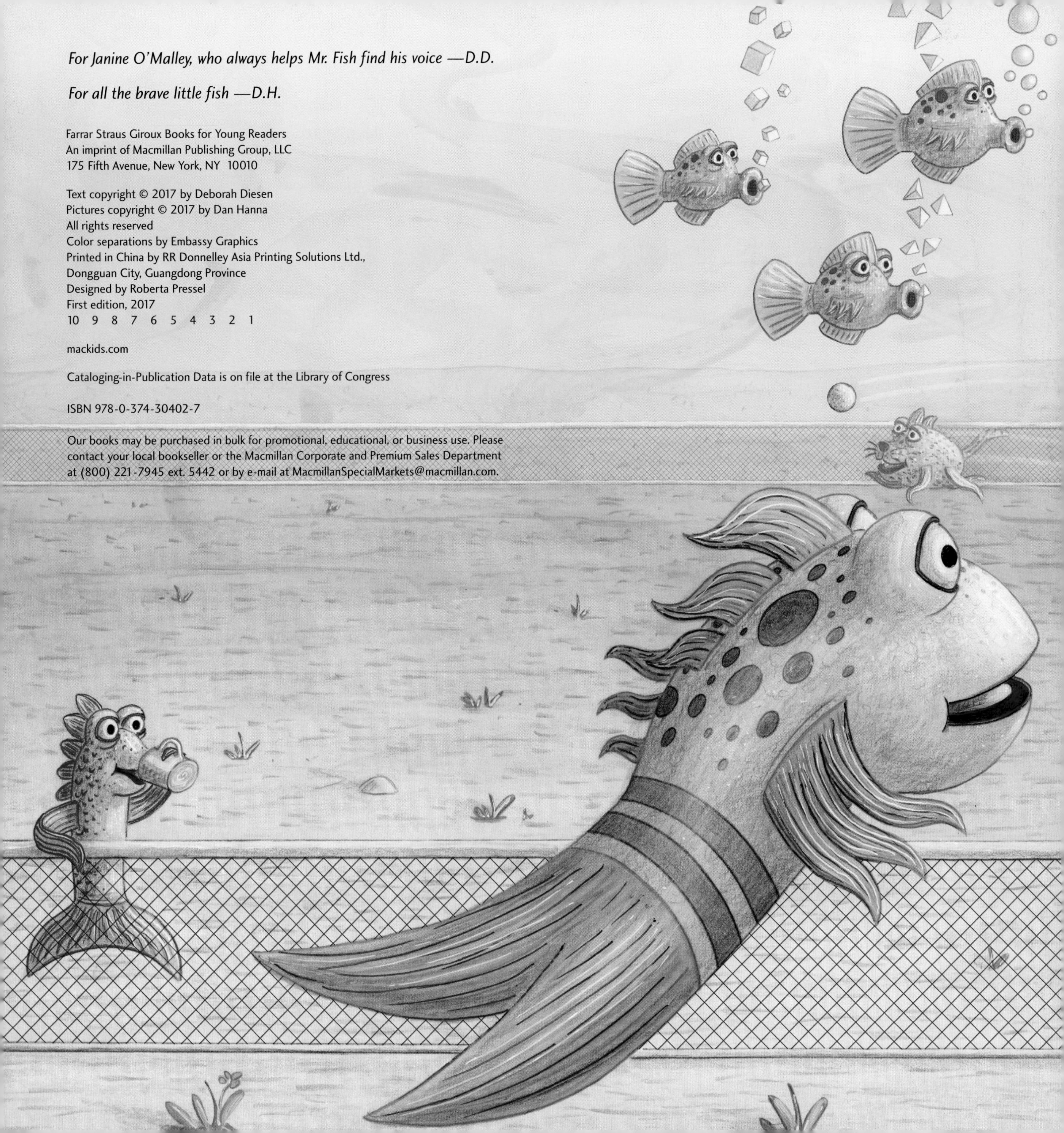

For Janine O'Malley, who always helps Mr. Fish find his voice —D.D.

For all the brave little fish —D.H.

Farrar Straus Giroux Books for Young Readers
An imprint of Macmillan Publishing Group, LLC
175 Fifth Avenue, New York, NY 10010

Color separations by Embassy Graphics
Printed in China by RR Donnelley Asia Printing Solutions Ltd.,
Dongguan City, Guangdong Province
Designed by Roberta Pressel
First edition, 2017
10 9 8 7 6 5 4 3 2 1

mackids.com

Cataloging-in-Publication Data is on file at the Library of Congress

ISBN 978-0-374-30402-7

Deep in the ocean
On a warm, gentle day
Bubbled lots of lovely laughter
And the sounds of happy play.

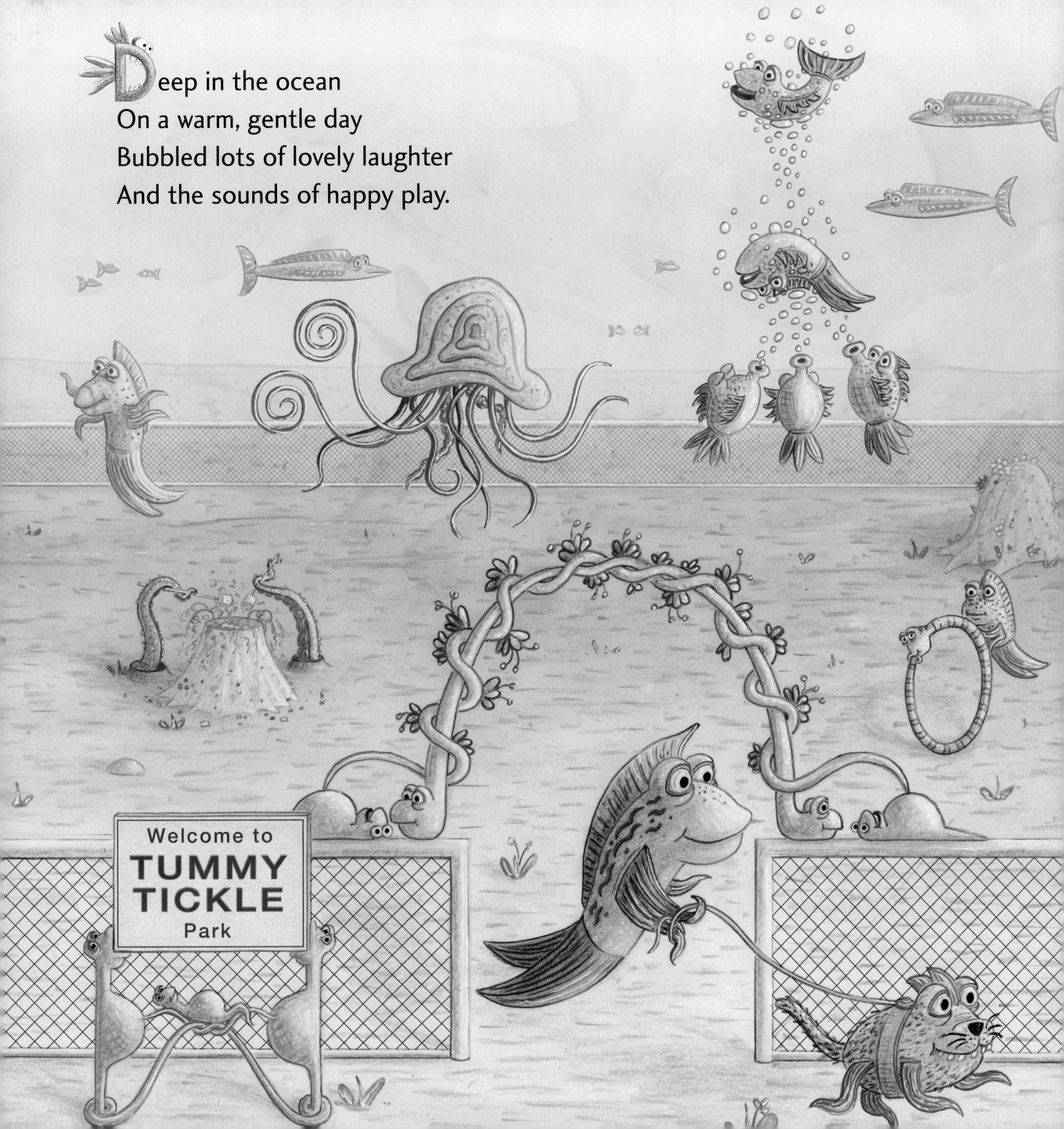
Welcome to
TUMMY
TICKLE
Park

Mr. Fish, his pals, and buddies
Were together at the park,

Having fun and feeling welcome,
When along came . . .

. . . a shark!

The shark showed his teeth,
And he growled as he swam.
"Move aside, micro-fishies!
It's *my* turn. **SCRAM!**"

Mr. Fish shrank back,
And he felt very strange.
The bright morning tilted
And the park began to change.

The friends all around him
Seemed to shrink back, too.
Mr. Fish's face flattened:
"Oh, I don't know what to do!

“Shark acted badly.
Being mean is *wrong*.
But I’m just one fish!
Am I really that strong?”

The water slowly calmed
And the friends found their way

Back to laughter-filled frolic
And a cheery-cheery day.

But the shark came ’round again!
And he used a bad name.
He shouted, “Get *lost*!
I’m the *boss* of this game.”

Mr. Fish shrank back
With his feelings in a lump.
Fear grew inside him
In a weird, heavy clump.

The friends all around him
Seemed to shrink back, too.
Mr. Fish's face furrowed:
"Oh, I don't know what to do!

Shark acted badly.
Being mean is *wrong*.
But I'm just one fish!
Am I really that strong?"

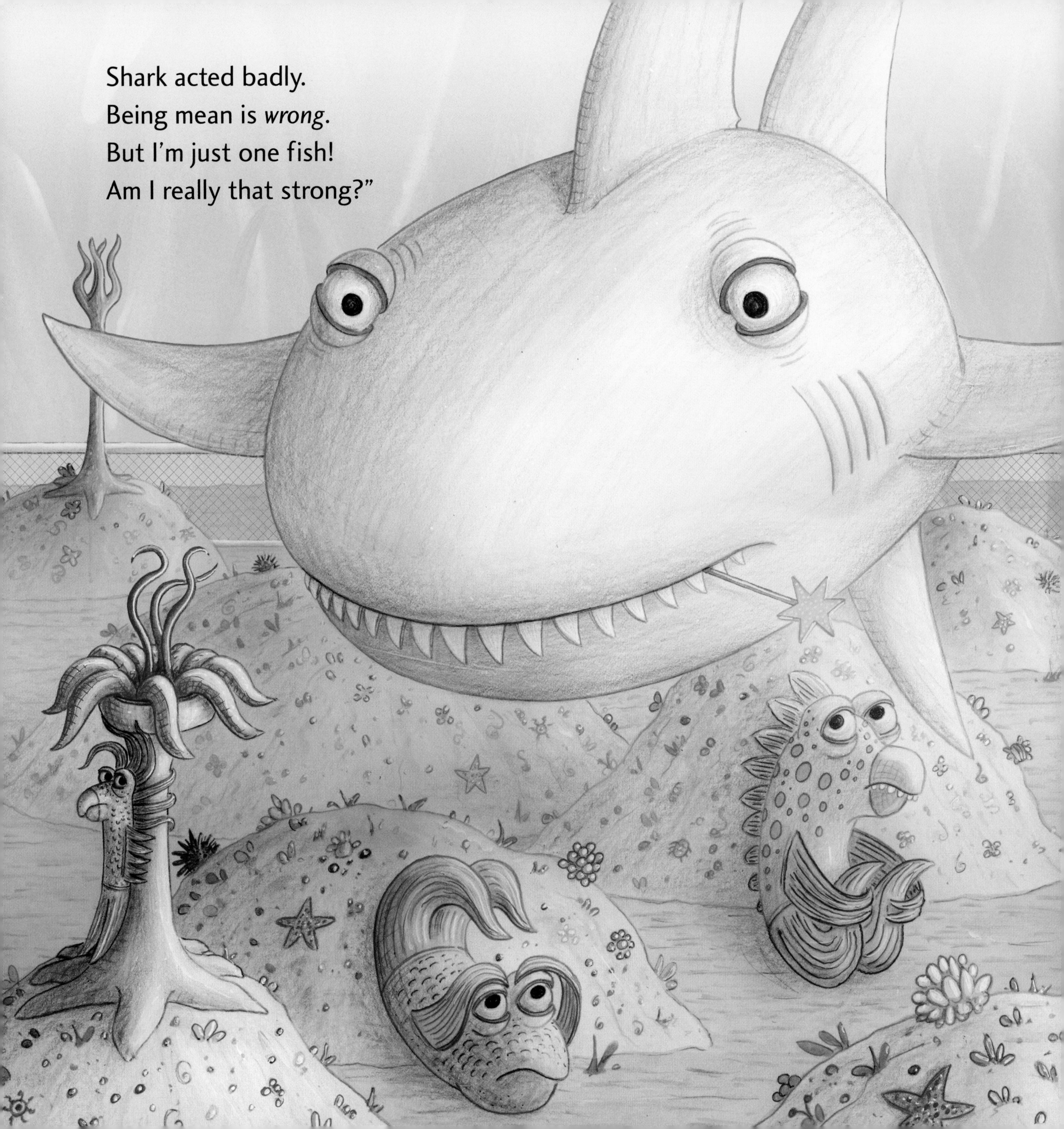

The friends tried again
To enjoy their favorite park,

But the shadow of their worries
Made the day seem dark.

The unmentioned tension
Grew when Shark reappeared.
He stole a guppy's lunch—
"Fear the *fin*!" he sneered.

Mr. Fish shrank back,
And his innards did a flop.
His feelings tumble-jumbled—
Would the awful ever stop?

The friends all around him
Seemed to shrink back, too.
Mr. Fish's face fizzled:
"Oh, I don't know what to do!

“Shark acted badly.
Being mean is *wrong*.
But I’m just one fish!
Am I really that strong?”

He turned to leave the park,
Feeling sad through and through.
Then slowly came a thought . . .
There was something he could do!

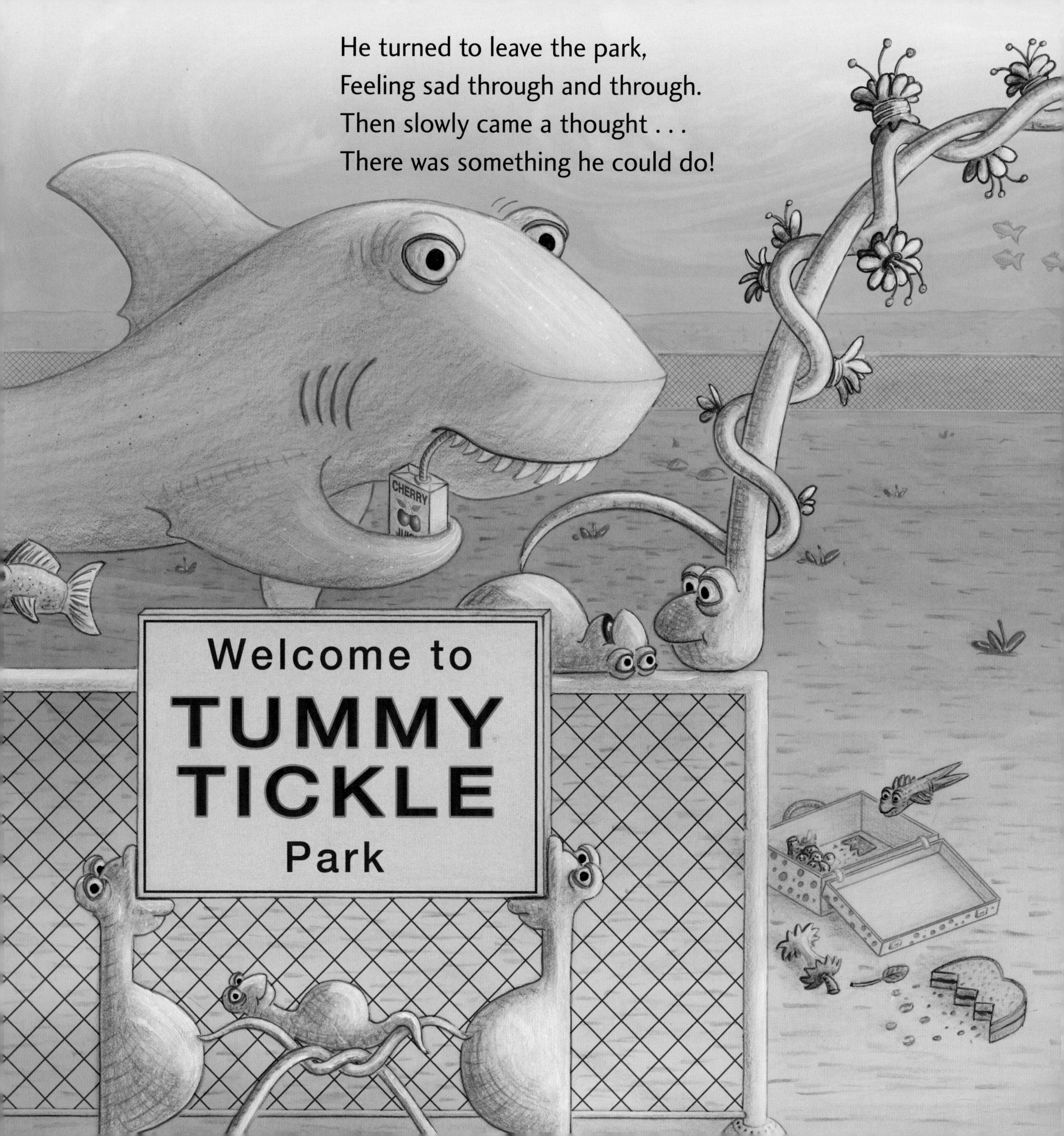
CHERRY
Welcome to
TUMMY
TICKLE
Park

"*Words* can make a difference
When things go wrong.
Yes, I'm just one fish,
But my *voice* is strong."

Mr. Fish turned back
And directly faced the shark.
It was time to talk straight
About what happened in the park.

"Mr. Shark," said Mr. Fish,
"You have broken up our fun.
Bully isn't who you *are*,
But it *is* what you have *done*.

“The things you did were mean,
And that’s not what we expect!
So please leave until you’re ready
To treat us with respect.”

As Mr. Fish spoke up,
And his words rang out loud,
The friends all around him
Formed an upstanding crowd.

Together they were stronger—
Now none of them were scared!
They *cared* about each other
And the ocean world they shared.

Soon Mr. Fish was laughing
And his friends were having fun,
Taking turns and using empathy
. . . *Each and every one.*

The park filled again
With the joyful sounds of play
Plus the confidence of knowing
How to keep it that way:

PARK RULES
1. Be kind.
2. Be fair.
3. If something goes wrong, SPEAK UP!
4. H
5. A
6. V
7. E
8.
9. F
10. U
11. N
12. !
SPARKLING SEAWEED JUICE

"We are kind. We are fair.
We are all potential friends.
So we speak up when we need to . . .

“That’s how bullying *ends*.”